my little Pony™

The Princess Promenade

adapted by Nora Pelizzari

HarperFestival®
A Division of HarperCollinsPublishers

"Spring is here! Spring is here!"
ZipZee could not wait to help plan the Spring Promenade.
"Is everyone ready?" she asked the other Breezies.
"It's time to go to Ponyville.
Wysteria is expecting us at the garden club meeting!"

It was Wysteria's favorite time of year. She loved to plan and prepare for the Spring Promenade with her friends. "Attention, everyone!" she called to the garden club members. "Our little friends the Breezies are here to help us with the promenade flowers and floats! Let's all go to the gardens."

At first, the gardening went well. But as soon as she saw the ugly weed in her flowerbed, Wysteria knew that she could not let it grow among her pretty flowers! Wysteria asked Pinkie Pie to help her dig it out. "Of course!" replied Pinkie Pie.

ZipZee watched as Wysteria and Pinkie Pie dug deeper and deeper.
"Yikes!" yelled Pinkie Pie. The Breezies gasped as Pinkie Pie and
Wysteria fell into the hole they were digging and disappeared.
"Oh, no! I'm going to follow them!" exclaimed ZipZee.

"Pinkie Pie! Are you okay?" Wysteria called into the dark tunnel.
"I'm fine," replied Pinkie Pie.
"What is that funny smell?" asked ZipZee.
"I don't know," said Wysteria, "but let's follow it
to see where this tunnel leads."

Pinkie Pie, Wysteria, and ZipZee stopped when they saw a
rare and beautiful flower growing out of a mound of dirt.
The odd smell seemed to be coming from under the flower.
While Wysteria was inspecting it, the pile of dirt started to shake.
"What is that?" cried Pinkie Pie.

It was a friendly little dragon! "I am Master Kenbroath Gillspotten Heathspike," he said politely. "Thank you for waking me up! And you may call me, simply, Spike."

"Hi, Simply Spike!" said ZipZee. "What are you doing here? What is that flower?"

"I have been sleeping for the last thousand years,"
he said as he handed Wysteria the beautiful flower.
"Now that you have woken me, the flower is yours," he told her.
"Oh, thank you!" said Wysteria. "Do you know how to get out of here?"
Spike smiled. "This tunnel leads to the Castle. Follow me!"

Meanwhile, the other ponies were getting worried. Sparkleworks and Sunny Daze were about to head into the tunnel to rescue their friends when they heard the drawbridge of Celebration Castle coming down.

The ponies all asked questions at once. Spike tried to answer them one by one. "Asleep for a thousand years, yes. Why am I here? Well, to guard the princess, of course!" The ponies told Spike that Ponyville did not have a princess. "You did not have a princess because I was asleep, but now that the princess has touched the flower . . ."

Pinkie Pie gasped. "Wysteria touched the flower!" she said.
Everyone looked at Wysteria. Spike bowed to his new princess.
"Princess Wysteria," he declared. "That sounds lovely."
"But I'm not a princess," said Wysteria.
"And I have a promenade to plan!"

"Princesses do not plan promenades. They ride in them," Spike told her.
"You have to start your princess lessons."
ZipZee zipped over to Wysteria. "I can plan the promenade for you,
Princess," she cried. "Please let me."
Wysteria smiled, "Well, okay. Thanks, ZipZee!"

Wysteria was busy learning how to be a princess. It was hard work!
Even walking wasn't as easy, but Wysteria tried her best.
"Now, Princess," said Spike, "for lesson number two,
what do your subjects call you?"
"But I don't have any subjects! I have friends," she said.

Oops! Wysteria took a bad step, and down fell the books.
Spike shook his head. He told her, "Princesses need subjects.
They don't need friends."
How sad, thought Wysteria. Being a princess
didn't seem as much fun without friends.

Outside of the Castle, the ponies were hard at work on the floats
for the promenade. ZipZee was flying from float to float,
trying to help as much as she could. Despite all of the hard work,
nothing looked quite right, even from ZipZee's bird's-eye view.
It just wasn't the same without Wysteria.

"I wish I could help with the promenade," said Wysteria.
"I want to smell the flowers and dig in the dirt."
Spike smiled and said, "Princesses do not smell flowers or dig
anything! They have subjects to do that." Wysteria had an idea.
"I've learned what it means to be a princess. Now I want to show you
what it means to be a pony," she told Spike.

"Princess Wysteria!" cried ZipZee. "You're here!"
Wysteria smiled. She said, "ZipZee, you have done a great job
on the floats, but I'd like to give them the royal treatment.
This year, it will be a Princess Promenade!"

At the promenade, all of Ponyville loved the beautiful floats.
Wysteria looked like a perfect princess on her special throne.
The ponies were surprised when she suddenly
stood up and called out, "Stop!"

Wysteria addressed the crowd. "I want to thank you all so much for making me feel so special as the first princess of Ponyville. As princess, I have a royal decree. I declare that each and every one of you is a princess, too!" And with that, all of the ponies became the Princesses of Ponyville . . . and Spike became the Prince!